DESPIC ME

THE JUNIOR NOVEL

Adapted by Annie Auerbach

Based on the screenplay by Cinco Paul & Ken Daurio

LITTLE, BROWN AND COMPANY
New York   Boston

Little, Brown and Company

Hachette Book Group
1290 Avenue of the Americas, New York, NY 10104
Visit our website at www.lb-kids.com

Little, Brown and Company is a division of Hachette Book Group, Inc.
The Little, Brown name and logo are trademarks of Hachette Book Group, Inc.

The publisher is not responsible for websites (or their content) that are not
owned by the publisher.

First Edition: May 2010

The characters and events portrayed in this book are fictitious.
Any similarity to real persons, living or dead, is coincidental and
not intended by the author.

ISBN 978-0-316-08380-5

10 9

RRD-C

Printed in the United States of America

PROLOGUE

"There is panic around the globe!"

— TV newsman

VROOM! A tacky tour bus rumbles through the Egyptian desert. A herder and his goats quickly jump out of the way as the bus zooms across the dunes, leaving behind clouds of dust. Inside the bus, a little boy with a skull and crossbones on his T-shirt lowers his sunglasses and presses his face against the window for a better look. His face bumps the window when the bus screeches to a halt. The little boy, named Justin, stumbles out tethered to a kid leash, with his mother holding on to the other end very tightly. All of the other tourists pile out, too, and stare in awe.

In front of them stands the Great Pyramid of Giza, the only remaining wonder of the Seven Wonders of the Ancient World.

Justin's father turns to his wife and holds up his hand. "Quick, honey, take my picture!" he says. "I got the pyramid in my hand!"

His wife snaps a few pictures. Then, through the viewfinder of the camera, she sees Justin running off into the distance. He has unhooked himself from the leash.

'You get back here right now!" she calls to her son.

Justin isn't listening. He is too busy crawling through the roped-off area that surrounds the pyramid. He holds a toy airplane in his hand and swoops it through the air, clueless to the danger he is getting into.

"No! Stop!" shouts a security guard.

"Do not cross the line!" another security guard yells.

The Egyptian security guards chase after Justin. The boy scampers up a rickety maintenance scaffolding.

"Wait, wait, wait! Hold on, little boy," the guard warns.

Justin just keeps playing with his toy airplane.

"Stop right there!" the other guard says, more urgently.

Justin turns back to look at the guards...and slips! He falls off the scaffolding, plummeting headfirst toward the pyramid!

Justin screams.

His mother screams.

KOOSH! Justin hits the pyramid—and then bounces off! He sails over the guards' heads. The tourists quickly snap pictures as Justin flies through the air, heading straight for his mother.

"I've got him! I've got him!" she screams frantically, tracking the boy's trajectory through the air.

With a *splat*, Justin lands right on top of his father. He's okay!

The pyramid, however, deflates like a big inflatable bounce house.

* * *

Word spreads quickly as newscasters report the day's biggest story.

"Outrage in Egypt tonight as it was discovered that the Great Pyramid of Giza has been stolen and replaced by a giant inflatable replica," says one newsman on the television.

The TV broadcast cuts away to footage of Egyptian police attempting to re-inflate the fake pyramid. It's going slowly. *Very* slowly.

The newscaster continues. "There is panic around the globe as countries and citizens try to protect their beloved landmarks."

The TV screen is flooded with footage of French police guarding the Eiffel Tower and Chinese tanks guarding the Great Wall.

"Law enforcement still has no leads, leaving the world to wonder: Which of the world's villains is responsible for this heinous crime? And where will he strike next?"

CHAPTER ONE

"Freeze Ray!"

— Gru

Gru is not the friendliest person you might meet. Instead, he's the type of person to give a sad child a balloon animal . . . and then promptly pop it. He's the type to pull up behind a cyclist on the road and blare his horn so loudly that the rider is blown from his bike. He is the type who doesn't wait in line for anything.

For instance, on this sunny day Gru walks into a local coffeehouse. When he sees the huge line of people, he's disappointed. Patience doesn't come easy for Gru. Inventive methods, however, do. Thinking quickly, he whips out a Freeze Ray. He points the weapon at the people in line and fires.

"Freeze Ray! Freeze Ray! Ha ha ha!" Gru laughs maniacally.

Everyone is instantly encased in blocks of ice. Gru grabs a full cup of coffee and a muffin from the woman who works behind the counter.

The thing is, Gru doesn't have a regular job like other people. He's a professional villain. So he drives an armored car, carries around a Freeze Ray, and lives in a big, scary house. In the middle of a typical street in typical suburbia sits Gru's very atypical home. It is all black— the roof, the siding, the door... even the tree in the front yard.

He walks through the living room, carrying his coffee and muffin. When he gets to the couch, he looks down over his long, pointy nose and frowns. Sprawled out on the couch is his pet dog, Kyle, who looks like a cross between a pit bull and a piranha. The dog is in Gru's spot, so the villain nudges him. The dog opens one eye and looks at his master. Then he closes it, going back to sleep. Gru nudges him again, a little harder. Kyle snores louder, clearly not going anywhere. Gru uses his foot to move the dog over and finally sits down to enjoy his coffee and muffin. He is about to turn on the TV when —

DING-DONG!

Gru sighs. He grudgingly gets up and goes to see who is at the front door. He looks through the peephole and grimaces. It's his next-door neighbor, Mr. McDade.

"Oh, hello, Fred," Gru says, opening the door.

"Hey, Gru," replies Mr. McDade. "I just wanted to talk to you about your house."

Still standing inside, Gru repeatedly pushes a button labeled TRAP DOOR, but it doesn't seem to be working. The front porch shudders, but Mr. McDade remains standing.

Mr. McDade chuckles nervously. "Ooh, gotta fix that porch," he says. Then he clears his throat and continues. "I just wanted to make sure you'd gotten the homeowners association notice about the unapproved exterior color, and the, uh, overall creepiness."

"Yes, I got it. It was wonderful," replies Gru. Then he slams the door shut.

"All righty, then," Mr. McDade says through the door. "Good seeing you, Gru."

A few minutes later, just as Gru raises the muffin to his mouth for a bite, the doorbell rings. Again.

Gru storms to the door, ready to let his neighbor have it. "Come on, Fred. Get a life, man!"

Before he opens the door, he hears a little girl's voice on the other side.

"Helloooo? Cookies for sale!"

Gru looks through the peephole and sees three little girls. They're selling Miss Hattie's Cookies—one of them carries a clipboard to write down orders.

"Go away," Gru says through the door. "I'm not home."

"Yes, you are," says Margo, the tallest girl. "I heard you."

"No, you didn't....This...is a recording," pretends Gru.

Margo isn't convinced. "No, it isn't."

"Yes, it is—watch this," replies Gru. "Leave a message. BEEP."

Margo and the other two girls, Edith and Agnes, turn to leave.

"Good-bye, recorded message!" Agnes calls, still standing at the door and clutching a stuffed unicorn.

"Agnes, come on," says Margo.

Finally returning to the couch, Gru turns on the TV. But instead of his favorite television show, the screen flashes the words INCOMING CALL.

Dr. Nefario's face fills the screen. The scientist works for Gru and is calling with some bad news.

"Gru, in spite of what happened today, to me you will always be one of the greats."

Gru just looks at Dr. Nefario in confusion. He has no idea what's going on.

"It's all over the news," Dr. Nefario explains. "Some guy just stole a pyramid!"

Gru attempts to process this information. Is this the end of his career? How could this happen? Then, the villain puts a determined look on his face. He's not going down without a fight!

CHAPTER TWO

"Assemble the minions!"

— Gru

Gru shuts off the television and runs to a large steel chair shaped like a giant rhino. That's right. A rhino. Horn and everything. He sits down and immediately presses a button on the remote control built into the rhino's leg. He is pushed forward, and a cannon hanging from the ceiling rotates and faces him. The cannon comes down and surrounds Gru, forming an elevator that leads to an underground lab. He spots a minion—one of his workers—and barks, "Assemble the minions!"

The minions are small yellow creatures who wear blue overalls and goggles. Some have only one eye. They work hard for their hero and creator, Gru.

Gru can hardly contain his anger as he heads toward the lab's center. In the massive steel lab there are numerous workstations. There's a minion break room, a minion gym, and even a minion water cooler. The minions have a whole world down there.

Passing it all by, Gru heads straight for the stage he has set up for his speeches. In a matter of minutes, all the minions have gathered. When Gru climbs up onstage, they can't contain their excitement. Applause and whistles echo throughout the underground lab.

"Hello, everybody!" says Gru, a lone spotlight illuminating him.

The minions explode with more cheers and screams. It's like a rock concert. "Gru! Gru!" they chant.

"Simmer down, simmer down," Gru says.

Finally, the minions quiet down. Gru takes a deep breath and makes an announcement: "Now, I realize that you guys probably heard about this other villain who stole the pyramid. Apparently it's a big deal. People are calling it the Crime of the Century and stuff like that."

Gru coughs and then continues. "But am I upset? No, I am not," he says. He sighs and adds, "Well, a little."

The minions look a bit sad.

Gru continues. "But we have had a pretty good year ourselves, and you guys are all right in my book."

A roar of applause erupts from the minions. Then one raises his hand.

Gru looks right at him and shakes his head. "No, no raises. You're not going to get any raises."

The minion shrugs and puts his hand down. He figures it didn't hurt to ask.

Attempting to boost morale, Gru shouts, "What did we do? Well, we stole the big screen from Times Square! Nice, huh? That's how I roll. Yeah, you all like watching football on that, huh?" He gestures to the giant screen that is hanging behind him.

"Wa-hoo!" shout the minions.

"But that's not all," continues Gru. He motions to his chief scientist, Dr. Nefario, a bald man with very large goggles and even larger ears. He wears a white lab coat and black rubber gloves.

"Thanks to the efforts of our very own Dr. Nefario," says Gru, "we have located a Shrink Ray in a secret lab."

The minions go crazy as the huge screen displays the Shrink Ray.

"Once we take this Shrink Ray, we will have the capability to pull off the true Crime of the Century. We are going to steal…"

The minions go wild, cheering and clapping.

"Wait, wait!" shouts Gru. "I haven't told you

what it is yet!" *ZOOSH!* One minion shoots a rocket off into the air. "Hey, Dave," Gru says, pointing to him. "Listen up, please."

Gru clears his throat and presses a button. The platform he's standing on begins to rise. "We are going to steal—*pause for effect*—the moon!" When his platform reaches its highest peak, he pushes another button, and a panel in the ceiling opens up, revealing the moon.

"And once the moon is mine, the world will give me whatever I want to get it back. I will be the greatest villain of all time. That's what I'm talking about!"

RIIIIING!

Gru furrows his brow as he pulls his cell phone out of his pocket. It's Dr. Nefario calling from down below. "Yes?"

Dr. Nefario's voice is very serious. "Gru, I've

been crunching some numbers, and I really don't see how we can afford this."

"Hey, chillax," replies Gru. "Don't poop on the party. I'm on this."

Dr. Nefario hangs up, wondering just what Gru has in mind....

CHAPTER THREE

"We wouldn't want
to spend the weekend
in the Box of Shame,
would we?"

— Miss Hattie

Meanwhile, in another part of town, the three little girls arrive home. Or at least it's their home for now. Miss Hattie's Home for Girls is the name of the orphanage where Margo, Edith, and Agnes live. They wish every day for a nice family to come and adopt each of them. They aren't technically sisters, but they spend all their time together. Margo is the oldest, Agnes is the youngest, and Edith is the messiest.

"Hi, Miss Hattie. We're back," announce the girls, standing behind a yellow line on the floor.

"Hello, girls," Miss Hattie says from behind her desk. She's surrounded by photographs hanging on the wall. Each one shows the face of an orphan staying at Miss Hattie's.

"Anybody come to adopt us while we were out?" Agnes asks, full of hope. She hooks a thumb through a strap of her overalls.

Miss Hattie cocks her head to one side. "Hmm. Let me think.... NO."

Despite the bad news, Edith places a ball of mud on Miss Hattie's desk as a gift.

"Edith! What did you put on my desk?!" exclaims Miss Hattie.

"A mud pie," Edith answers proudly. The pink knit hat that she wears bobs in excitement.

Miss Hattie looks Edith right in the eyes. "You're never going to get adopted, Edith. You know that, don't you?"

Edith's hat droops. "Yeah, I know," Edith says with a shrug.

"Good," replies Miss Hattie. She really isn't that good with children. Switching the subject, Miss Hattie asks the girls how the cookie selling went. "Did we meet our quotas?"

"Sorta," replies Margo. "We sold forty-three Minty Mints, thirty Choco Swirlies, and eighteen Coconutties."

Miss Hattie is not pleased. She gets up from

her desk and paces the room. "You say that like it's a great sale day."

Margo looks at the other two girls.

"LOOK AT MY FACE!" bellows Miss Hattie. "Do you think it's a great sale day?!"

Taking a deep breath, Miss Hattie tries to regain her composure. "Eighteen Coconutties . . . I think we can do a little better than that, don't you? Yeah, we wouldn't want to spend the weekend in the Box of Shame, would we?"

The three girls look at the turquoise tile floor. "No, Miss Hattie," they say in unison.

"Good," Miss Hattie says. "Off you go. Go clean something of mine."

The girls shuffle off, passing by a cardboard box that has been labeled BOX OF SHAME with a marker. There is a small hole cut out on one side.

"Hi, Penny," say the girls.

"Hi, guys," replies Penny from inside the cardboard box.

* * *

That night, Margo, Agnes, and Edith kneel together in their tiny room, saying their prayers.

"...And please watch over us and bless us that we'll have a good night's sleep," Margo says.

"...And bless that while we're sleeping, no bugs will crawl into our ears and lay eggs in our brains," adds Edith.

Margo shoots her a disapproving look. "Great. Thanks for that image."

Agnes continues with the prayers. "...And please bless that someone will adopt us soon... and that the mommy and daddy will be nice... and have a pet unicorn. Amen."

"Amen," say Margo and Edith.

The girls climb into their beds, and Margo turns out the light. Agnes begins singing to her stuffed unicorn, which goes with her everywhere:

"Unicorns, I love them,
Unicorns, I love them,
Uni, uni, unicorns, I love them."

Edith puts her pillow over her head. But Agnes keeps on singing.

"Uni, unicorns, I could pet one,
If they were really real.
And they are!
So I bought one so I could pet it.
Now it loves me, now I love it,
La la la la la la."

While she sleeps, Agnes dreams of unicorns. She also dreams of being part of a family…as she does every night.

CHAPTER FOUR

"There are a lot of new villains out there."

— Mr. Perkins

"Hello, Mom. To what do I owe this pleasure?"

Gru is in his car when he receives a call from his mother, the meanest woman on the planet. She is in the middle of a karate class.

"I just wanted to congratulate you on stealing the pyramid," his mother says. "That was you, wasn't it? Or was it a villain who's actually successful?"

Gru clenches his teeth. "Why is it that nothing I ever do is good enough for you?"

Gru's mother stops mid-kick and stares at the phone through her cat's-eye-shaped glasses. "That is so not true."

"It is true!" insists Gru. He can remember when he was a child. He drew a picture of his mother and proudly showed it to her. She just shrugged and went back to reading her book.

So he made a statue of her out of pasta. Noodles were piled high to represent her tower of hair. He painted a massive portrait of her as the

Mona Lisa. Each time, she wasn't impressed in the least.

A determined look crosses Gru's face. "Just so you know, Mom," he begins. "I am about to do something very, very big—very important. When you hear about it, you will be very proud."

In her karate class, his mother simply shrugs. "Okay, I'm out of here."

Gru sighs. It seems that no matter what he does, he can't please his mother. But that doesn't keep him from trying. It's time to put his next big plan in motion. A wicked grin crosses Gru's face as he drives down the street toward the bank. Right in front is a small parking space between two cars. *SMASH!* He knocks one out of the way. *CRASH!* He demolishes the other one.

Holding his briefcase, Gru casually gets out of his car and walks inside the bank. He strides past the receptionist and into the restroom.

After using his Freeze Ray on the only other guy in there, Gru stands in front of a urinal. Lasers shoot out of it, scanning Gru's eyes. A secret door opens, and Gru enters the Bank of Evil— the secret underground bank that finances all of the world's villains.

Gru walks down a hallway featuring a series of statues of a man being progressively crushed by a pillar. He has always liked that work of art.

Soon he arrives at the Loans Desk. "Gru to see Mr. Perkins," he says to the receptionist.

"Yes, please have a seat," replies the receptionist.

Gru takes a seat on a red leather sofa. He unrolls a piece of paper with his master plan to steal the moon. As he studies it, something distracting catches his eye. He looks up to see a nerdy villain sitting across from him. The villain wears glasses and a costume that looks like an orange tracksuit, but with a really big collar. His potbelly is not part of the costume.

"Hey," says the other villain.

Gru doesn't say a word and goes back to studying his plan. The villain comes and sits down next to Gru.

"I'm applying for a new villain loan," he says to Gru. "I go by the name of Vector."

Irritated, Gru slides to the other end of the couch. Vector follows.

"It's a mathematical term," Vector says of his name. "A quantity represented by an arrow with both direction and magnitude."

Gru attempts to ignore him. Vector doesn't seem to notice.

"Vector. That's me. 'Cause I'm committing crimes with both direction and magnitude. Oh, yeah!"

Gru continues to pay no attention to him, so

Vector holds up a futuristic-looking gun with a dangerous piranha sloshing around inside the barrel. The sharp-toothed fish gasps for air.

"Check out my new weapon: Piranha Gun!" brags Vector. "Oh, yes! It fires live piranhas at you. Ever seen one before? No, you haven't—I invented it." Vector's eyes light up as he gets an idea. "You want a demonstration?"

Before Vector can even aim the weapon, the piranha falls out of the barrel and onto the floor, flopping around. Vector tries to catch the slimy creature. "Oh...ah...! So difficult sometimes to get the piranha back in my—"

Gru wishes he could be anywhere else at the moment. He finds it painful watching this pathetic wannabe villain and his ridiculous Piranha Gun. Luckily, at that moment the receptionist speaks up.

"Mr. Gru? Mr. Perkins will see you now."

Thrilled to escape from the ramblings of Vector, Gru springs off the couch. He follows the receptionist into the office of the loan manager, Mr. Perkins. The large man has hair shaped like horns, and he sits behind an enormous desk.

Excitedly, Gru makes his presentation to Mr. Perkins. He sets up charts, showing how he plans to use a Shrink Ray to shrink the moon and steal it. One diagram even shows the rocket he'll use.

"So all I need is some funding from the bank, and then the moon is ours," Gru finishes, and sits down. He holds his breath, hoping to get enough money at least to build the rocket.

"Wow. Well, very nice presentation," Mr. Perkins says. "I'd like to see this Shrink Ray."

Gru squirms in his seat. "Absolutely. Will do," he tells Mr. Perkins. Then quietly, he adds, "As soon as I have it."

Mr. Perkins frowns. "You don't have it?" he asks. "And yet you have the audacity to ask the bank for money?"

"Apparently," Gru agrees, with a nod.

Mr. Perkins's voice begins to rise. "Do you have any idea of the capital that this bank has invested in you, Gru? With far too few of your sinister plots actually turning a profit, I might add." Mr. Perkins stands up and walks around his office. "Hmm...how can I put it?" He pulls an apple from his coat. "Say this apple is you. If we don't start getting our money back..."

Mr. Perkins squeezes the apple until it explodes!

"Get the picture?" says Mr. Perkins with a nasty grin as he shakes the apple juice off his hand. Then he holds up a balloon that is filled with something.

"What about this convenient balloon filled with flour? Let's say this is you." Mr. Perkins hurls the balloon at the wall, where it bursts in a shower of white powder.

Gru gulps loudly.

"Look, Gru, the point is, there are a lot of new villains out there. Younger than you. Hungrier than you. Like that young fellow out there named Vector. He just stole the pyramid."

Gru's eyes widen. That incompetent guy he met in the lobby had stolen the pyramid?

Hastily, Gru tries to bring the conversation back to himself. "So, as far as getting the money for the rocket…?"

"Get the Shrink Ray," Mr. Perkins tells him. "Then we'll talk."

Feeling defeated, Gru trudges out of Mr. Perkins's office and into the lobby. There, he sees Vector trying to stick the piranha back into his gun. Gru looks around and then casually pulls out his Freeze Ray and freezes Vector's head.

Stunned, Vector moves his eyes to look at Gru, before his body falls over onto the floor. As Gru walks away, he sees the piranha jump on top of the now defenseless Vector. Gru smiles to himself. Now about that Shrink Ray...

CHAPTER FIVE

"Now maybe you'll think twice before you freeze someone's head!"

— Vector

On the far side of the globe, on a top secret island, in a top secret facility, a top secret experiment is under way. A worker pushes a cart through the halls and into a lab. On the cart sits the coveted Shrink Ray. The worker picks up the futuristic-looking weapon and places it in the center of the testing room. Opposite the Shrink Ray stands an elephant. The animal has no idea what it's doing there, but it doesn't have a good feeling.

From behind a window, two scientists in green lab coats look in. All around them are flashing lights and monitors constantly scrolling data. One scientist nods to the other, and then a switch gets flipped.

The Shrink Ray begins to hum, and lights flash. It is charging up. The scientists look excited. Things are looking good! Then the Shrink Ray hums louder and begins to glow. The scientists grab each other. This is it!

FZZZZCHEEWWW! A bolt of energy shoots out and hits the elephant across the room. The huge animal suddenly shrinks down to the size of a mouse! It makes a meek, high-pitched trumpet sound.

The scientists embrace and dance around ecstatically until they hear... *VZZZHHHT!*

The scientists look up to see a laser cutting a large circle in the ceiling of the lab. It's Gru! His massive aircraft hovers just above the hole. Within seconds, one of his minions rides down on a giant claw. The minion grabs the Shrink Ray from its stand and then smiles arrogantly as the claw is retracted.

"Ha ha! Suckers!" says the minion. He isn't looking where he's going and bumps his head on the ceiling. "Ow!"

He repeats, "Suckers!" and tries to exit again. But he still doesn't make it through the hole. Minions are great for some things; making a dramatic exit is not one of them. Finally, he lines the claw up correctly and goes up through the hole to the waiting aircraft that Dr. Nefario designed for Gru.

As the plane takes off into the sky, the claw places the Shrink Ray and the minion into a glass case. Gru and another minion celebrate their success until they hear... *VZZZHHHT!*

A laser cuts a hole in the plane's ceiling, right above the Shrink Ray. A *different* giant claw enters Gru's aircraft and grabs the case with the Shrink Ray! The claw shakes the case until the minion falls out.

Gru and the minions are stunned. Gru turns to look out the front window and exclaims, "What? No no no no!"

A larger white ship hovers above. It belongs to Vector, the ridiculous villain from the bank.

Vector yells down to Gru. "Mwa-ha-ha! Now maybe you'll think twice before you freeze someone's head!" Now in possession of the Shrink Ray, Vector blasts off.

"Quick! We can't let him get away!" Gru tells his minions.

The chase is on. Gru orders a minion to fire a machine gun. But all the bullets miss Vector's ship. Gru engages all the rockets he has on board and fires. But Vector easily avoids every one of them.

"How adorable," Vector mocks.

Gru clenches his jaw and lines up another shot. "Got you in our sights. Like taking candy from a—"

Gru is speechless as he watches Vector stand on top of his ship. He's aiming the Shrink Ray directly at Gru and his minions!

"Hey, Gru, try this on for size!" Vector says with a wicked laugh.

ZZZZTTTT! Gru's ship starts to shrink! Gru's seat belt shrinks so much that it breaks.

"This is claustrophobic," says Gru, struggling as the ship continues to get smaller and smaller around him and the minions.

Vector laughs victoriously and takes off with a roar of the engine.

By this time, Gru's ship has flipped upside down.

"Too small," groans Gru. "This is too small for me."

Gru and the minions are squeezed out the front of the cockpit like toothpaste. Gru holds on to the upside-down ship as the minions grab his legs. Finally, they right the ship, but they struggle to keep their balance on top of the now tiny aircraft.

"I don't like that guy," Gru mutters as the ship coasts down toward the ground.

CHAPTER SIX

"I'm going to need a
dozen tiny remote-
controlled robots that
look like cookies . . .
Cookie Robots!"

— Gru

Gru is not a villain who gives up easily, and he is certainly not someone who admits defeat to a nerd like Vector. So Gru puts his next plan into action. Dressed in a disguise with a wig of dreadlocks and a knit hat, Gru walks a mechanical puppy down the street where Vector's house is located. The house is more like a fortress, with a huge white dome and a wall protecting all sides of it. A security camera atop the wall rotates and tries to focus in on Gru. He leaps backward and pins himself flat against the far side of the wall.

After a moment, nothing bad happens, so Gru activates the puppy into periscope mode. The dog's mechanical head rises and peers over Vector's wall.

Inside, Vector lounges on his couch playing video games. A shark and a school of fish swim beneath the glass floor. Yeah, it's a pretty cool fortress.

Suddenly a security alert blares. Vector clicks a tiny remote, and a monitor shows the spying puppy periscope. Vector puts down the video game controller and picks up a much larger remote control. He pushes a button. Instantly, a large laser gun emerges from the dome atop his lair. It fires—burning the puppy periscope to a crisp!

Gru groans and tries to get into the fortress another way. He just *has* to get that Shrink Ray back. After all, he stole it in the first place!

But it isn't easy. When Gru tries to pole-vault over the wall, mechanical boxing gloves repeatedly hit him. When he uses a jetpack to fly up and land on the roof, a giant catapult flings him right back. He tries to scale the wall, but giant saws slice through his ropes. The shark even pops out of a manhole and bites him! Every way that Gru tries to get into Vector's fortress, he's thwarted.

That doesn't stop Gru from returning the next day. He still has no luck getting inside, but you have to give him points for his determination.

While Gru sits across the street, bruised and battered from his latest failed attempt, he sees three girls approach the fortress and ring the buzzer.

"Good luck, little girls," he laughs bitterly.

Gru puts a pair of binoculars to his face and watches as the security cameras activate.

One girl speaks into the camera. It's Margo. "Uh, hi. We're orphans from Miss Hattie's Home for Girls."

"I don't care. Beat it," Vector says through the intercom.

"Come on, we're selling cookies, so, you know, we can have a better future," Margo explains.

"Oh, wait, wait...do you have Coconutties?" asks Vector, suddenly nice.

'Uh...yeah," replies Margo.

VHHHRRRT! The gates open, allowing the girls to enter the fortress.

Back in the crater, Gru has a wonderfully devious idea: he can use the girls to get the Shrink Ray from Vector's lair!

Gru flips open his cell phone and dials. "Dr. Nefario? I'm going to need a dozen tiny remote-controlled robots that look like cookies...Cookie Robots."

With newfound hope, Gru laughs. What *sweet* revenge!

CHAPTER SEVEN

**"Here's
the dealio."**

— Gru

Miss Hattie sits behind her desk, checking her computer screen. Across from her sits Gru, wearing an all-white dentist's outfit, complete with rubber gloves.

"Well, it appears you've cleared our background check, Dr. Gru. Oh, and I see you have made a list of some of your personal achievements. Thank you for that; I love reading."

Miss Hattie has no idea that back in Gru's lab, a minion has hacked into Miss Hattie's computer and is at that very moment typing random information into the file.

Miss Hattie continues to read. "And I see you've been given the Medal of Honor... and knighthood...and the Nobel Prize for Dentistry."

More and more details pop up on her screen as *many* minions are now typing different ideas. They're fighting each other to get to the keyboard.

"You run marathons. You had your own cooking show?" asks Miss Hattie. At that moment, her computer screen goes haywire with tons of random information. "What in the name of...?"

Gru knows he has to do something before his cover is blown. "Here's the dealio. Things have been so lonely since my wife, Debbie, passed on." He starts to act emotional. "It's like my heart is a tooth, and it's got a cavity that can only be filled with children." He puts his head in his hands, trying to contain his emotions.

Looking up, he realizes that his approach isn't working on Miss Hattie. Apparently, she isn't the emotional type. It's time for him to change his tactics.

"You are a beautiful woman," he murmurs. "Do you speak Spanish?"

Miss Hattie gives him a blank stare. "Do I look like I speak Spanish?"

"You have a face *como un burro*," Gru says tenderly.

Miss Hattie giggles. "Oh, well, thank you."

She doesn't know he actually said she has a face like a donkey! But Gru doesn't care, as long as he can carry out his master cookie caper. "Can we proceed with this adoption?" he presses.

Miss Hattie pushes a button on her intercom. "Please tell Margo, Edith, and Agnes to come to the lobby."

As soon as the girls hear, they run to their tiny room to pack their suitcases. The three girls scream and jump for joy.

"I bet the mama's beautiful," says Margo.

"I bet the daddy's eyes sparkle," says Edith.

"I bet their house is made of gummy bears," says Agnes.

The other two girls give Agnes a strange look.

"I'm just saying it'd be nice," Agnes says with a shrug.

Then they frantically run to the lobby.

"Girls, I want you to meet Mr. Gru. He's going to adopt you. And he's a dentist," explains Miss Hattie.

Gru stands and turns to the girls, who stare up at him. He could not be farther from their ideal image of adoptive parents.

Margo does the introductions. "Uh, hi. I'm Margo. This is Edith. That's Agnes."

Agnes runs to Gru, wrapping herself around his leg. Gru attempts a smile. It works. Sort of. Then he shakes his leg, trying to shake Agnes off. "Okay, that's enough, little girl. Let go of my leg. Come on."

Agnes won't budge.

"How do you remove them?" Gru pleads with Miss Hattie. "Is there a command? Some non-stick spray? Crowbar?"

In the end, Gru shuffles out with Agnes still attached. The girls pile into Gru's car, and he peels out of the driveway. Margo notices that they crunch a little kid's wagon underneath a tire. She looks over at Gru in alarm, but he just smiles.

It doesn't take long to drive to Gru's house. "Here we are. Home sweet home," Gru says.

The girls stand outside and gaze at the large black house. It doesn't look friendly. It doesn't look homey. And it certainly doesn't look like a place for three little girls. Margo and the other two huddle close together, with worried looks on their faces.

Then Margo remembers something. "Wait a second. You're the guy who pretended he was a recorded message." She *knew* the house looked familiar.

Gru opens the front door. "No, that was some-one else," he says dismissively.

Margo raises her eyebrows, unconvinced. She follows the others inside. They look around, taking in the scary-looking interior. Frightening images are everywhere.

Agnes feels very nervous. "Can I hold your hand?" she asks Gru.

"Ah...no," Gru replies.

Just then Kyle comes bounding around the corner. His eyes light up when he sees the girls. He licks his chops and is about to chomp down on Agnes with a slobbery mouth full of teeth when Gru stops him with a swat from a rolled-up newspaper.

"No, Kyle!" commands Gru. "These are not treats. These are guests." He turns to the girls. "This is Kyle, my...dog."

"Oooh, fluffy doggie!" Agnes coos.

That sends Kyle running scared the other way.

"What kind of dog is that?" Margo asks.

"He's a...a...I don't know," answers Gru.

Since Margo is the oldest of the girls, she feels it is her responsibility to look after the other two. "Do you really think this is an appropriate place for little kids?" she demands. "'Cause, uh, it's NOT."

Gru shrugs and leads the girls to the kitchen. He points to a dog dish filled with candy and another one with water. Newspapers are spread out on the floor.

"As you can see, I have provided everything a child might need," he says.

The girls just stare at him. Is he serious?

Gru proceeds. "We need to set up some rules. Rule number one: you will not touch anything."

"What about the floor?" asks Margo.

Gru sighs with irritation. "Yes, you may touch the floor."

"What about the air?"

"Yes, you may touch the air."

"What about this?" asks Edith, holding up a dangerous Ray Gun.

"Ahhh! Where did you get that?" Gru screams, shielding himself with a frying pan.

"Found it," Edith says with a shrug.

Gru grabs the Ray Gun from her. The girls are already ignoring rule number one!

Moving on, Gru tells them rule number two: "No bothering me while I'm working."

Then there is rule number three: "You will not cry or whine or laugh or giggle or sneeze or burp or fart. So no, no, no annoying sounds. All right?"

"Does this count as annoying?" asks Agnes as she opens her mouth and drums on her cheeks.

"Very," answers Gru. He heads for the door. "I will see you in six hours."

After Gru slams the door, the girls stand

there in silence. Margo sees the somber faces on the other girls and tries to cheer them— and herself—up.

"Don't worry. Everything's going to be fine," Margo says. "We're going to be really happy here. Right, Agnes?"

Agnes is on all fours eating candy out of the dish like a dog. She looks up. "Hmm?"

Margo smiles. It seems Agnes is adapting to her new home just fine.

Too bad the girls have no idea what Gru's real plans for them are.

NEWS FLASH! The Great Pyramid of Giza has been stolen and replaced by a giant inflatable replica.

Law enforcement still has no leads, leaving the world to wonder: Which of the world's villains is responsible for this heinous crime? And where do you hide a pyramid?

Is the thief Gru? Not this time!

But Gru does have a Freeze Ray and other cool gadgets!

Gru gives Vector the cold shoulder.

He's just jealous that Vector stole the pyramid.

Gru's new master plan requires stealing a Shrink Ray.
The minions help him out!

"Ha ha! Suckers!"

That Shrink Ray really works! "Toot!"

"Success! The Shrink Ray is ours! Mwa-ha-ha!"

That pesky villain Vector steals the Shrink Ray from Gru.
To get it back, Gru breaks in to Vector's fortress.

Gru readies himself for any booby traps.

SPLAT! The high jump doesn't work.

Vector has a serious alarm system . . .

. . . and a shark!

Gru concocts a new plan that requires three
little girls . . . but little girls need bedtime stories,
ballet lessons, and a trip to Super Silly Fun Land!

Kyle thinks guests are snacks! "Grrrr!"

CHAPTER EIGHT

"Don't let the bedbugs
bite, because there are
literally thousands
of them."

— Gru

Gru stares at a collection of miniature robots on a table in the lab. Each robot has one eye, a metallic underbite, and a giant wig of curly hair. Next to them stands Dr. Nefario, his chest puffed out with pride. Disco music blares through the speakers, and the little robots start to dance. They're actually pretty good!

Looking confused, Gru asks, "Uh, what are these?"

Dr. Nefario grooves to the beat and says, "A dozen Boogie Robots! *Booogieee!*"

Gru grabs the remote control and pushes the stop button.

"*Cookie* Robots!" cries Gru. "I said Cookie Robots!"

Dr. Nefario's mouth drops open. Whoops.

"Okay, I'm on it," the scientist says, feeling quite embarrassed.

* * *

Meanwhile, the girls are upstairs exploring the dark and ghastly house. They wander into the main room.

"TV!" Agnes cheers. She tries to climb up on the rhino chair and accidentally steps on the remote control in the chair's leg. The cannon drops down from above, revealing the secret entrance.

"Whoa, this is cool! Come on!" says Edith. The other girls follow out of curiosity.

"I don't think he's a dentist," Agnes says as they ride down in the elevator to the secret lab.

* * *

Back inside the lab, Dr. Nefario presents a normal-looking cookie on the table. This is no ordinary cookie, however. With a *vzzzzrt*, mechanical legs emerge from the sides of the cookie and it stands up, looking like a robotic spider with a chewy center. The cookie scampers across the table toward Gru, who smiles.

"Congratulations," Gru says to Dr. Nefario. "Now, *those* are Cookie Robots! We are one step closer to getting that Shrink Ray and ultimately...the moon!" He and the scientist exchange high fives.

Suddenly a toy unicorn appears from behind the table. A tiny hand makes it hop along.

"La la la la la. I love unicorns. I love unicorns. If they were real, I could pet one," sings Agnes.

Gru grits his teeth as the three girls emerge from behind the table.

"What are you doing here? I told you to stay in the kitchen," he says.

"We got bored," answers Margo. "What is this place?"

Gru isn't sure how to answer, so he ignores the question. "Get back in the kitchen."

"Will you play with us?" Agnes asks innocently.

"No."

"Why?"

"Because!" Gru replies. "I'm busy!"

"Doing what? 'Cause I don't see any patients here. Or dental equipment," Margo points out.

"Um, okay, okay, you got me," says Gru. "The dentist thing is more of a hobby. In real life, my job is…a spy. I am a spy. And it is top secret, and you may not tell anybody."

Edith isn't listening. "What does this do?" She pushes a button, and a laser shoots out from a panel in the wall.

"No! Don't touch that!" shouts Dr. Nefario.

It's too late. The laser makes contact with Agnes's stuffed unicorn. The stuffed animal instantly turns to ashes.

"Waaaaaah!" cries Agnes.

"That is an annoying sound," Gru says to her. "Remember our deal?"

"Waaaaaah!"

"Okay, we get it. You're sad," says Gru. "Now stop it!"

Margo shakes her head. "She's not going to stop. That was her favorite unicorn."

Gru feels like he might explode from the piercing cries. Thinking quickly, he calls over some of his minions.

"This is a code red," Gru explains. "I need you to go and get the girl a new toy. And hurry!"

The minions salute and run off.

"Who are those little guys?" Margo asks.

"They are my...uh...cousins," Gru replies. "Okay, bedtime."

"Awww," the girls whine, following Gru to their bedroom.

Once the girls see their new bedroom, they stop and stare. The beds are actually three nuclear warhead casings, with a pillow and blanket nestled inside each one.

Without wasting another moment, Gru plops each girl into a bed. "Okay, all tucked in. Sweet dreams," he says.

"Just so you know," begins Margo, "you're never going to be my dad."

"I think I can live with that," Gru replies.

Margo is taken aback by Gru's response. It isn't what she expected, and she feels a little sad.

Agnes holds up a book and asks Gru to read them a bedtime story. When Gru refuses, Agnes says, "But we can't go to sleep without a bedtime story."

Without missing a beat, Gru says, "Well, then, it's going to be a long night for you, isn't it?"

That leaves Agnes speechless. Did he really just say that?

"Good night, sleep tight," he continues. "Don't let the bedbugs bite, because there are literally thousands of them. Oh, and there's probably something in your closet." He walks out of the girls' room, shutting off the lights and closing the door.

"He's just kidding, Agnes," says Margo. But none of the girls are convinced.

Then the door opens, and three minions enter. One of them approaches Agnes and hands her the new "toy." It's a toilet brush that the minions dressed up to look like a unicorn.

Agnes smiles. "It's beautiful," she says, giving one minion a kiss.

The minion blushes and they leave the room.

Agnes closes her eyes and goes to sleep, clutching the toilet brush all night.

CHAPTER NINE

"Welcome back
to the Fortress
of Vectortude."

— Vector

"Girls, let's go! Time to deliver cookies!"

Gru has loaded up all the cookies, including his special Cookie Robots, into a wagon.

The girls come out the front door wearing ballet tutus.

"First we're going to dance class," insists Margo.

Gru shakes his head. "Actually, we're going to have to skip the dance class today."

"*Actually*, we can't skip the dance class today," Margo tells him. "We have a big recital coming up. We're doing a dance from *Swan Lake*."

"That's fantastic, wonderful," Gru says dismissively. He heads for his van. "But right now we're going to deliver cookies."

"No," says Margo.

"No?" repeats Gru, a little surprised.

"We're not going to deliver cookies until we go to dance class," Margo says firmly. She folds her arms. Edith does the same. Agnes has a little trouble folding her arms, then finally gets it. Then the three of them start marching down the street.

Gru fumes with anger. "You just keep walking!" he yells. "Because I'm not driving you!"

Margo calls back over her shoulder, "Okay."

A few minutes later, Gru is in his car, driving slowly alongside the girls. "I am going to give you to the count of three, and if you're not in this car...I can't even tell you what. One, two, two and three-quarters...two and seven-eighths... I am serious! I'll make it five. But that's it. Five looms in your future."

Fifteen minutes later, Gru finds himself sitting in the waiting room, along with the other parents. While the girls take their class, Gru is forced to hold all the girls' girly stuff: dolls, clothes, and anything pink. He looks miserable.

When the class ends, Agnes runs up to him. "Here you go," she says, holding out a ticket.

"What is this?" asks Gru.

"Your ticket to the dance recital," explains Agnes. "You're coming, right?"

"Of course, of course," replies Gru, totally lying. "I have pins and needles that I am sitting on."

Wide-eyed and hopeful, Agnes holds up her pinkie to him. "Pinkie promise?"

Gru stares at her. He notices that the other girls are watching them. Realizing he will do whatever it takes to get those cookies delivered, Gru reluctantly holds out his pinkie. "My pinkie promises."

Finally, after the dance class detour, Gru gets the girls back in the van to begin his master plan to steal back the Shrink Ray. He parks down the street from Vector's fortress and begins to stack cookie boxes in a wagon on the sidewalk. The girls change into their clothes and join him.

"Our first customer is a man named Vector," Gru says.

Margo looks at her order form. "But he's a *V.* We're supposed to start with the *A*'s, then we go to the *B*'s, then we go to the—"

"Yes, yes," interrupts Gru. "I went to kindergarten. I know how the alphabet works!" Realizing he's being too harsh, Gru quickly softens and says, "I was just thinking that it might be nice to deliver Mr. Vector's first, that's all."

The girls nod and make their way down the sidewalk toward Vector's fortress.

Gru suppresses a smile and repeats to himself, "It's almost over....It's almost over." He goes inside the back of the van and watches the girls on a video screen.

The girls enter the gate, and Vector greets them at the front door. "Ah, girls, welcome back to the Fortress of Vectortude." He laughs and then leads them inside.

Margo consults her order form as Edith and Agnes put Vector's twenty-three boxes of cookies on the counter, including the Coconut-ties box with the robotic cookies in it. Inside the van, Gru launches Cookie Robot software on his computer so he can control the robotic cookies.

"That will be fifty-two dollars," Margo tells Vector.

Vector zips open his fanny pack and looks for money. He doesn't notice that twelve robotic cookies are climbing out of the box and scampering across the counter behind him.

The cookies quickly run a scan of the house and locate the Shrink Ray in a vault. They leap off the counter and scurry down the hall. They form a ladder to reach the security panel beside the vault and then shut down Vector's security system.

The vault door slowly opens, revealing the Shrink Ray. The Cookie Robots happily high-five each other. But they can't carry the Shrink

Ray out the front door—they are too small! Gru, of course, knows that. So he instructs them to go to the far side of the vault and burn a hole in the wall. Gru and two minions climb in through the hole.

Meanwhile, Vector counts out the money and hands it to Margo.

"Why are you wearing your pajamas?" Agnes asks him.

"These are not pajamas. This is a warm-up suit," Vector answers, slightly annoyed. He leads the girls out, with no idea of the Shrink Ray robbery happening in his own home.

But the robbery hits a snag. While Gru and his minions struggle to lift the heavy Shrink Ray case, the Cookie Robots accidentally seal up the hole in the wall. They're all trapped inside!

CHAPTER TEN

"It's so fluffy!"

— Agnes

Stuck inside Vector's fortress, Gru has to think fast. He orders the minions to help him lift the heavy Shrink Ray into an air duct. One minion grabs the other minion and shakes him until he glows. Now they have light in the duct! The threesome crawls through the air duct, dragging the Shrink Ray behind them.

To his relief, Gru spots a way out ahead. But he never makes it there. Since the Shrink Ray is so heavy, they all fall through a weak spot in the floor of the duct, and through the ceiling of Vector's living room! They dangle dangerously above Vector, who is watching TV. Although Vector is oblivious to what's going on above him, his pet shark is not so clueless. Swimming beneath the glass floor, the shark notices the tender morsel above that is Gru.

The shark lunges, striking the glass hard.

"What the . . . ?" Vector wonders. "Quiet down, fish."

THUMP! The shark strikes the glass again, causing the whole room to shake. Gru and his minions are knocked from their position — but so is Vector, who ends up with his head in a bucket of snacks. He never sees Gru and the minions make a break for it. They don't want to be the shark's lunch!

Gru meets the girls back by the van. He hurries them inside.

"But what about all the other people who ordered cookies?" Margo asks.

"Life's full of disappointments . . . for some people," Gru replies, and begins driving.

At that moment, Agnes sees something out the window and screams. Gru swerves as he tries to figure out what is wrong.

"Super Silly Fun Land!" Agnes explains,

pointing to the amusement park. "Can we go? Please?"

The other girls join in. "Please? We'll never ask for anything else ever again!"

Gru stares at the girls, then smiles as a plan forms in his head. "Okay," he says finally.

He leads them into the amusement park and watches as they climb into a roller coaster car.

"Come on," Edith calls to him.

Gru shakes his head. "Good-bye! Have fun!"

A park worker turns to Gru and says, "Sorry, dude, they can't ride without an adult."

"What?" asks a surprised Gru. "Ugh." His plan to ditch the girls is foiled!

Gru is stuck riding the roller coaster with the girls. There are loops; there are corkscrews; there are giant drops. The girls are ecstatic, but Gru... not so much. By the end, he looks beaten and battered and ready to throw up.

As they walk by the shooting-gallery booth, Agnes screams again. She points to the main prize—a unicorn. "It's so fluffy, I'm going to die!" she cries.

"You *have* to let us play for it," insists Margo.

"No no no," says Gru.

The girls beg again. A heavy sigh escapes Gru's lips, and he turns to the vendor in the booth. "How much for the fluffy unicorn?"

"It's not for sale," replies the sleazy-looking vendor. "But all you have to do to win it is knock down that little spaceship there." He points to the smallest of the spaceship targets.

Gru nods and slaps a one-dollar bill on the counter. The girls then take aim and fire. They all miss.

The next time they try, Agnes actually hits the target! "I hit it! Did you see that? I hit it!" she sings.

But when they are told that Agnes didn't actually win, Gru steps in. "She hit that. I saw that with my own eyes," he says to the vendor.

The vendor gives a smarmy smile. "Hey, buddy, you see that little tin spaceship? See how it's *not* knocked over? That means you didn't win!"

Gru's blood begins to boil. "Okay, my turn," he says, reaching into his coat pocket. He pulls out a small device that transforms into an enormous Ray Gun.

TCHEW! A bright blue bolt connects with the back of the shooting range. There's nothing left of the tiny spaceship targets—just a gaping hole.

Gru turns to the vendor. "Knocked over!"

The vendor trembles, his hair smoking from the blast. He doesn't protest as Gru pockets the weapon, grabs the unicorn, and hands it to

Agnes. Margo and Edith cheer, and Agnes hugs the animal tight.

"It's so fluffy!" exclaims Agnes again.

"That was awesome! You blew up the whole thing!" Edith and Margo say.

"Let's go destroy another game!" suggests Agnes.

And then the most incredible thing happens: Gru allows a small smile to creep across his face.

★ ★ ★

Later that night, Gru and the girls return home. They all laugh and chat about the day's excitement. Gru's arms are full of souvenirs from Super Silly Fun Land.

Inside the house, they all see Dr. Nefario waiting for them. He doesn't look happy.

Gru turns to the girls and says, "Okay, girls, go play."

The girls obediently run off with their goodies. Gru turns back to Dr. Nefario.

"I got the Shrink Ray," Gru says lightly.

Dr. Nefario continues to simply stare.

Gru holds out a treat. "Cotton candy?"

Dr. Nefario bristles. "We have twelve days until the moon is in perfect position, Gru. We can't afford any distractions."

Gru nods seriously and says, "Get me Perkins on the video phone."

CHAPTER ELEVEN

"I fly to the moon.
I shrink the moon.
I grab the moon."

— Gru

"Sorry to bother you, Mr. Perkins, but I figured that you would want to see this."

"What?" says Mr. Perkins. He and Gru are having a videoconference. Each has a video camera that projects his image to the other person's TV.

Gru aims the Shrink Ray at a minion and fires it, and the minion shrinks! In fact, it's so tiny that another minion flicks the shrunken minion through the air. Gru catches the screaming minion in midair and looks back at Mr. Perkins's image on the TV screen.

Mr. Perkins looks amazed. "Well done, Gru. Rather impressive."

Gru smiles. Everything is finally going his way! He reaches for a set of slick art boards set up on an easel, using them to illustrate his plan:

"I fly to the moon. I shrink the moon. I grab the moon. I sit on the toilet. Wait, WHAT?!"

The fourth board is a child's drawing of Gru sitting on the toilet. It is signed by Edith.

Gru tries to contain his anger. He looks at the camera and says, "Sorry, sorry. Would you excuse me for just one second?"

Mr. Perkins frowns as Gru slips out of sight. Gru storms over to the girls, who are giggling in the doorway.

"I told you not to touch my things. I told you a thousand times!" Gru whispers angrily.

"Uh-huh," says Margo distractedly. "Can we order pizza?"

"Pizza? You just had lunch," says Gru.

"Not now, later. For dinner," explains Edith.

"Fine, fine, whatever," says Gru. "Just get back in there."

"Ooh, can we get stuffed crust?" asks Margo.

"I'll stuff you all in the crust!" he says, trying to keep it together.

Agnes giggles. "You're funny."

"Just don't come out of that room again!" insists Gru. He shuts the door and rushes back to the video monitor and smiles.

"All right. Sorry about that. Where were we?"

Mr. Perkins looks irritated. "You were sitting on the toilet."

"No no no! No, I'm sorry," Gru says quickly.

Suddenly Gru hears a noise and glances toward the door. It's open again. Uh-oh.

"You don't seem terribly focused, Gru," says Mr. Perkins.

"Believe me, I am completely focused," Gru insists.

Just then, the girls' faces pop up on the TV screen.

"What are those? Children?!" Mr. Perkins splutters.

"Are we on TV?" asks Agnes.

Gru rushes after the girls. "Argh! What are

you doing? I told you to stay out of here!" He chases the girls out and turns back to Mr. Perkins to speak. But then the girls run in again with the Freeze Ray and zap Gru. His whole body except for his head and two hands is encased in a block of ice. He rocks back and forth to scoot in front of the screen. "As I was saying—"

Mr. Perkins cuts him off. "No need to continue. I've seen quite enough."

"But my plan was—" begins Gru.

"I love everything about your plan," Mr. Perkins says. "Except for one thing: you."

Gru stares at Mr. Perkins, confused. "I don't understand."

"Let's face reality, Gru. You've been at this far too long with far too little success," Mr. Perkins explains. "We're going to put our faith and money into, well...a younger villain. One who actually might make something of himself."

Gru is stunned and struggles for words.

"It's over," says Mr. Perkins. "Good-bye, Gru."

* * *

With a heavy heart, Gru walks back into the lab and addresses the minions.

"Now, I know there have been some rumors going around that the bank is no longer funding us. Well, I am here to put those rumors to rest. They are *true*."

The minions react with shock and horror. Margo, Edith, and Agnes hear the announcement, too. They exchange looks and then run off.

Gru continues. "In terms of money...we have no money. So how will we get to the moon? The answer is clear: we won't." Gru drops into an empty chair, defeated. The crowd becomes even more disheartened. "We are doomed.

Now would probably be a good time to look for other employment options. I have fired up my résumé, as I suggest that all of you do, as well."

The crowd sighs collectively. Gru feels horrible, as if he's let everyone down. Then he feels a tug on his jacket. He looks down and sees Margo, Edith, and Agnes. He frowns.

"What is it? Can't you see I am in the middle of a pep talk?" he grumbles.

Agnes holds out a piggy bank. Puzzled, Gru takes the piggy bank and shakes it. He opens it, and several coins fall out into his hand. He looks at the girls, surprised by the feelings he's having.

Then, one by one, the minions produce their own treasured possessions: wallets, wads of money, a mounted fish.

Gru looks at everyone and all the contributions. A smile forms on his face. "Yes!" he decides. "Who needs the bank? We will build our own rocket, using this and whatever else we can find!"

* * *

Gru crosses out a date on his wall calendar. A ticket that says DANCE RECITAL is clipped to the same day that says STEAL THE MOON. But he doesn't pay much attention. He has a rocket to build—and fast!

Dr. Nefario is hard at work putting together the rocket. Also hard at work are the girls, practicing their ballet for the recital. A few of the minions like to practice with them, too. When Gru first sees all of them dance, he watches with interest...until Dr. Nefario spots him. Gru quickly changes his look to one of disapproval.

Launch day is getting closer. Gru crosses off another square on his calendar. That afternoon, he enters the living room to find a surprise: his mother sitting on the couch with the three girls! They are looking through an old scrapbook.

"And there he is in the bathtub," Gru's mother says, pointing to a picture.

The girls giggle.

Gru is mortified. "Mom! What are you doing here?"

His mom ignores him and just points to another picture. "And here he is all dressed up in his Sunday best."

"He looks like a girl," says Margo.

Gru's mother laughs. "Yes, he does. An ugly girl."

Gru shakes his head. He can't believe his mother is there spending time with the girls! He goes back to the lab, shaking his head in disbelief.

Finally, after much hard work, the rocket is

finished. Dr. Nefario is ready to unveil the completed rocket, which is a hodgepodge of different parts.

But Dr. Nefario can't find anyone in the lab. The scientist is furious. He storms into Gru's house and finds Gru showing off by making pancakes for the girls. Gru does not see Dr. Nefario becoming enraged behind him.

Dr. Nefario thinks the girls are ruining all the plans. And he thinks they're ruining Gru, too. After all, what kind of villain enjoys *cooking*?

CHAPTER TWELVE

"Victor was
my nerd name.
Now I am Vector."

— Vector

Mr. Perkins sits at his desk, smashing various items. First he crushes a coconut. Pleased with the way it flattens, he moves on to a lightbulb. He is reaching for a stuffed toad playing a guitar when the receptionist enters.

"Mr. Perkins? Your son is here," she announces.

His face falls. Then he says, "Send him in."

The receptionist leaves, and then through the door steps...Vector!

"Hi, Dad. You wanted to see me?" he says, acting as if everything is okay.

Mr. Perkins nods. "Yes, I did, Victor."

"I am not Victor anymore. Victor was my nerd name. Now I am Vector."

With a steely gaze, Mr. Perkins tells him to sit down.

Mr. Perkins raises his eyebrows. "Do you know where the Shrink Ray is?"

"Duh, back at my place," replies Vector.

"Really?" says his father. "Then I guess Gru must have one that *looks exactly like it*!" He flips open his laptop, which displays a freeze-frame from the videoconference. It shows Gru holding the Shrink Ray. In the background are Margo, Edith, and Agnes.

Vector gasps at the image. "Those girls sold me cookies!"

Mr. Perkins looks intently at his son. "Do you have any idea how lucrative this moon heist could be? I gave you the opportunity of a lifetime, and you just blew it!"

Vector tries to figure out a way to save face. "No, I didn't," he lies.

"Really?" his father asks.

"Just wait till Gru sees my latest weapon: Squid Launcher. Oh, yeah!" Vector pulls out his Squid Launcher and fires it out the door.

"Aaaaiiiggghhh! There's a squid on my face!"

screams the unfortunate employee the squid landed on.

Vector turns back to his father and declares, "Don't worry. The moon is as good as ours."

CHAPTER THIRTEEN

"This is no place for children."

— Dr. Nefario

"Come on, it's bedtime!" Gru tells the girls.

Margo, Edith, and Agnes are running around all over the place.

"Did you brush your teeth?" asks Gru. "Put on your PJs. Hold still! Seriously, seriously! This is beddy-bye time. Right now. I am not kidding around. I mean it!"

"But we're not tired," Edith says.

"Well, *I* am tired!" Gru says.

Agnes holds up a copy of a book titled *Sleepy Kittens*. "Will you read us a bedtime story?"

"No," says Gru.

"Pretty please?" begs Agnes, pouting her lips and making big sad eyes.

"The physical appearance of the 'please' makes no difference," Gru points out. "It is still no. So go to sleep."

"We can't. We're all hyper," says Edith.

Margo smiles. "And without a bedtime story,

we'll just keep getting up and bugging you. *All night long.*"

Gru sighs. "Fine." He takes the book from Agnes and sits down on the floor next to the girls' beds. He opens the book, revealing three kitten finger puppets attached to it. "What are these?"

"Puppets," explains Agnes. "You use them when you tell the story."

Gru is intrigued. He sticks three of his fingers through the back of the book to wiggle the finger puppets, and then he begins to read:

> *Three little kittens started to bawl,*
> *"Mommy, we're not tired at all."*
> *Their mother smiled and said with a purr,*
> *"Fine, but at least you should brush your*
> *   fur."*

"Now you brush the fur," instructs Edith.

There is a little brush attached to the page. Gru picks it up and brushes the kittens' fur.

"This is literature? A two-year-old could have written this," he grumbles. He turns the page and continues reading:

Three little kittens with fur all brushed
said, "We can't sleep, we feel too rushed."
Their mother replied with a voice like silk,
"Fine, but at least you should drink your
            milk."

"Now make them drink the milk," Agnes says.

Gru makes the puppets drink milk from the saucer illustrated on the page. He turns to the next page and notices that Agnes has snuggled up next to him. He moves her arm so it isn't so close to him.

Three little kittens with milk all gone,
rubbed their eyes and started to yawn.

All three girls yawn, as does Gru.

"Good night kittens, close your eyes.
Sleep in peace until you rise.
Though while you sleep, we are apart…
your mommy loves you with all her heart!"

Tears well up in Gru's eyes. The girls look up at him, surprised by his reaction. Realizing what's going on, Gru immediately slams the book shut.

"The end. Okay, good night!" says Gru, running for the door.

"Wait!" yells Agnes.

Gru stops. "What?"

"What about good night kisses?" she asks.

Gru tries to keep his emotions contained as he responds. "No no no! There will be no kissing or hugging!" Then he leaves.

"I like him. He's nice," Agnes says to the other girls.

Edith nods and adds, "But scary."

"Like Santa," says Agnes.

In the hallway, Gru tries to regain his composure. He walks past the framed family tree on the wall and does a double take. On the wall below the frame, the girls have drawn themselves in with crayons, to make themselves part of the family. Gru has a moment of yearning before he hears...

"Only forty-eight hours until the rocket launch, and all systems are go!" exclaims Dr. Nefario.

Gru nervously begins to pick up after the girls—shoes, socks, toys, even crackers are scattered about. "Um, about that. I was thinking maybe we could move the date of the heist."

Dr. Nefario is taken aback. "What? Why?"

"No reason," Gru says, trying to act casual. "I just thought that—"

Dr. Nefario puts his hands on his hips and squares his jaw. "Is this because of the girls' dance recital?"

"No no no! The recital? No," Gru replies quickly. "I just think it's kind of weird to do it on a Saturday. I was thinking maybe a moon heist is more of a Tuesday thing."

But Dr. Nefario isn't buying Gru's excuse. "That's it! You are on the verge of becoming the greatest villain of all time, Gru. 'The Man Who Stole the Moon'!"

"I know," Gru says quietly.

"These girls are becoming a major distraction,

and there is absolutely no reason to keep them here."

Gru can't believe what he is hearing.

"They need to go," Dr. Nefario adds cruelly. "If you don't do something about it, I will."

CHAPTER FOURTEEN

*"I am the greatest
criminal mind
of the century!"*

— Gru

The next day, Gru is having a tea party with the three girls when the doorbell rings. He opens the door to see Miss Hattie on the other side. "What are you doing here?" he asks.

"I'm here for the girls," she replies. "I received a call that you wanted to return them."

Gru is stunned. He never placed that call!

"I also purchased a Spanish dictionary," continues Miss Hattie. Then she slaps Gru across the face with it. "I don't like what you said!"

At that moment, Gru hears someone behind him clearing his throat. He turns to see Dr. Nefario across the room. He gives Gru a thumbs-up. Gru is shocked that Nefario has made good on his promise. The scientist had called the orphanage.

Feeling utterly trapped, Gru soon realizes he has no choice. He turns back to Miss Hattie and mutters, "I'll get the girls ready."

A little while later, Gru carries the girls' bags to the car. Despite the girls' eyes welling up with tears, Gru does his best not to let any feelings show.

Suddenly, Agnes grabs Gru's leg. "Don't let her take us back, Mr. Gru," she pleads. "Tell her that you want to keep us."

Gru wants to respond, but he can't do it. The disappointment he sees in the girls' faces devastates him.

Miss Hattie snorts. She's had enough of this nonsense. "All right, girls. Come on, let's go."

Gru watches the car drive away, his heart breaking.

Happy to see the girls leave, Dr. Nefario is ready to get back to business. "I did it for your own good. Now, let's go get that moon!"

Gru looks at him but just can't summon up the same degree of excitement. Dr. Nefario watches as Gru heads back into the house, clearly depressed. From the windows, the minions watch as well, sobbing uncontrollably.

That day Gru sees the girls everywhere he turns. He picks up the dolls they have left behind. He watches the minions clean the wall where the girls drew themselves below the family tree. Finally, in an effort to stop feeling so blue, Gru throws himself into his mission to steal the moon.

With his space suit on, Gru walks through his lab and stops to look up at the rocket. He has to admit that it *is* impressive. Along with a minion, he rides a lift to the top of the rocket. The minion hands him something.

"What is this for?" asks Gru. He looks down and realizes it is a ticket for the dance recital. He pushes down his true feelings and yells, "I am the greatest criminal mind of the century! I don't go to little girls' dance recitals!"

Gru throws the ticket in the air and turns back to the rocket, ready for the moon heist. What he doesn't see is that the minion has caught the ticket and has secretly stuck it into one of Gru's space suit pockets.

Stepping into the hatch, Gru sits in his seat in the cockpit and fastens his seat belt. Dr. Nefario appears on a video monitor. "Opening launch bay doors," he tells Gru.

KA-CHONG! A slit of sunlight appears through the cockpit window as massive hangar doors open overhead. Dr. Nefario begins the count-down on the video monitor.

"Commencing launch sequence, and we are good to go in T-minus ten seconds. Ten... nine... eight... seven..."

The rocket rumbles, and smoke whirls all around the engines.

"Six... five... four... three... two... one!"

Lifting off, the rocket soars into the air. Down

on the ground in Gru's backyard stands a surprising spectator: Vector! Gru's nemesis immediately pulls out his Squid Launcher, aims it at the rocket, and fires.

SPLAAAT! The squid connects with the rocket and sticks to it. It is attached to a line, which is attached to Vector. The line quickly takes up slack and *whoosh*! Vector is yanked into the sky after the rocket.

The rocket tears through the sky toward space with Vector still attached. He climbs up the line to the rocket and looks through the window. "Boo-yah!" he says, startling Gru.

Once Gru recovers from his shock, he pushes down the toaster button on the control panel. Now the whole rocket is electrically charged.

"Aaaaiiigghhh!" screams Vector as he is blown off the rocket. He falls through the air, heading straight for the ground far below. Is this the end for Vector?

CHAPTER FIFTEEN

"But he pinkie
promised!"

— Agnes

Vector plummets back toward Earth. Then he remembers he's wearing a flight suit! He pulls a ripcord, and sails unfurl on either side of his suit, making him look like a flying squirrel. A very large, very ugly flying squirrel. The wind catches the sails, and Vector soars across the sky.

"Oh, yeah!" he shouts triumphantly. "Once again, the mighty Vector—"

SPLAT! He smacks right into an electrical tower. Stunned, Vector slides to the ground.

* * *

Gru's rocket begins to glow, burning hotter as it reaches the edge of Earth's atmosphere. Gru holds on for dear life as the rocket violently shakes and rumbles. The view through the cockpit window changes from blue to purple to the blackness of space. Suddenly the shaking stops, and everything is still. Gru looks out the window at the moon in the starry distance. He smiles.

He maneuvers his rocket closer and powers down the engines. The ship silently hovers above the lunar surface. Gru pushes a button, and doors open. He holds the Shrink Ray in his hands and faces the enormous moon. Gru can't believe how large it actually is. But it won't be large for long!

ZZZZZZEEEET! A bolt of energy fires from the Shrink Ray and engulfs the moon. Then slowly it begins to shrink. Gru reaches out to grab the tiny moon. It's the size of a baseball!

"Ha! I've got it! I've got the moon!" he shouts. Not bogged down by gravity, Gru does a flip and floats around jubilantly in his space suit. Then his mood shifts and his smile fades. Somehow, having the moon isn't as satisfying as he thought it would be. Silently floating in the vastness of space, Gru feels small and alone.

Just then, something drifts out of his pocket. It's the ticket to the dance recital. Gru stares at it and feels overwhelmed. He really wants to see the girls. He checks his watch. "I can make it," he says with determination.

Back on Earth, the changes are immediate. Without the moon, surfers suddenly lose their waves. A werewolf howling at the moon changes back to a man.

Worse, however, is what happens in the lab. Dr. Nefario watches the rocket on his monitor and then turns to see the tiny minion that had suffered a blast from the Shrink Ray begin to grow! Within seconds the minion returns to its normal size! Uh-oh!

"Wait a minute. How...?" Dr. Nefario starts. He runs to a door and opens it. He sees that the spaceship Vector shrunk is now back to its original size, too. "Oh, no."

Dr. Nefario grabs the radio. "Gru? Gru, can you hear me? The Shrink Ray effects are only temporary!"

But Dr. Nefario hears only static. Gru's ship has reached the edge of Earth's atmosphere, and the radio isn't working. Gru pushes hard on the throttle to try to get to the dance recital on time.

On the ground, Dr. Nefario thinks for a moment. "We've got to warn him! Let's go!" he says to the minions, and they all rush out of the lab.

* * *

Decorations cover the entrance to the dance studio. Margo, Edith, and Agnes peer out from behind the curtain, dressed in their ballerina costumes. Agnes sees the empty chair in the audience. "He's still not here," she says sadly to the other girls.

"Why would he come? He gave us up," Margo points out.

"But he pinkie promised!" cries Agnes.

"Girls, places!" calls the dance teacher.

"No, we can't start yet!" insists Edith. "We're still expecting someone!"

Agnes looks up at the teacher with her best puppy dog eyes. "Can we just wait a few more minutes?"

The dance teacher sighs. "All right. But just a few more minutes."

When she has left, Margo turns to the other girls. "He's not coming, guys," she says.

Edith and Agnes look shaken. Could it be true?

After a few minutes, the dance recital has to begin. The lights dim, and classical music plays over the speakers. The curtains open and all the girls come out dancing. All the dancers wear big smiles except three girls at the far left—Margo, Edith, and Agnes. They look sad.

Everyone in the audience turns on a video camera. Except for one person: Vector.

CHAPTER SIXTEEN

"Sorry, buddy.
Show's over."

— A janitor

Gru looks down at the city below, trying to locate the dance studio. "Okay, okay, there's the library...that's Third Street, that's the dance studio! There it is!"

With a final thrust, the spaceship touches down in the middle of the street. The tires screech and smoke as pedestrians dive out of the way. Gru slams on the brakes, and with a *thoomph* the brake parachute activates.

Gru unfastens his seat belt and races out of the ship and into the dance studio. He stops suddenly as he sees the empty hall.

"Sorry, buddy. Show's over," says a janitor who is taking down the folding chairs.

Gru can't believe it. Then something catches his eye. He makes his way over to a chair in the front row and removes a sign taped to it. Written in a child's handwriting, it says MARGO, EDITH, AND AGNES'S DAD.

Crushed, Gru stares at the paper. He flips

it over and discovers that Vector has left him a note. He turns and races out of the dance studio.

Gru makes his way as fast as possible to Vector's fortress.

"Vector! Open up!" Gru demands, pounding on the front gate.

A huge TV monitor appears over the gate. Vector's face ripples into view. "First give me the moon. *Then* we'll talk," he says.

Gru holds the shrunken moon up to the monitor.

A suction hose extends from the side of the monitor. It hovers in the air, waiting for the moon. Then from behind Vector, Agnes calls out, "Mr. Gru!"

"Zip it," Vector tells her.

That's all it takes. Gru's heart lurches to hear someone be mean to Agnes. He places the moon near the end of the hose, and it gets sucked in.

The hose promptly retracts into the building. On the monitor, Gru watches as the hose delivers the moon to Vector.

"Now the girls," demands Gru.

Vector grins wickedly. "Actually, I think I'll hold on to them for a while longer."

Gru sees the monitor retract back inside the building and disappear.

"No!" yells Gru. He grits his teeth and speaks into a security camera. "Listen closely, you little punk. You have no idea who you are messing with, and when I get in there, you are going to be in a world of pain!"

Inside, Vector stares at the monitor. "Oh, I'm really scared," he says, laughing.

At that moment, Gru punches the camera so hard, the lens cracks. Vector jumps, which makes the girls smile.

Confidently, Gru begins his march to rescue the girls. *BAM!* He kicks down the gate. *POW!*

A mechanical boxing glove aims for him. After a few of Gru's best karate moves, the glove is worthless. *WHOOSH!* The shark jumps out of the water at him. With one punch, Gru knocks the beast back into the water.

Vector watches all of it on another monitor... and starts to panic.

Gru is about to kick down the final door when the entire fortress starts to rumble. Suddenly, the room lifts off, detaching itself from the rest of the building. It's an escape pod! Gru grabs the side of the escape pod as it soars into the air.

CHAPTER SEVENTEEN

"This time, good
triumphs. Who is this
mysterious hero?
And what will he
do next?"

— TV Newsman

Gru holds on as tight as he can while the escape pod flies through the sky. Gru is relieved when he soon sees Dr. Nefario piloting his own airship next to the pod, coming to Gru's rescue.

Then it dawns on him. "The ship's big again?"

"Not as big as the moon is going to be," explains Dr. Nefario.

Gru looks out the cockpit window and sees Vector's escape pod zooming away in the distance. "Oh, no, the girls!" They hurry after it.

Inside Vector's pod, the scoundrel sticks Margo, Edith, and Agnes inside a giant glass bubble. Then he looks through the rearview mirror and sees Gru's ship approaching. Vector pushes the throttle forward and tries to get away. He doesn't notice the moon wobble and increase to the size of a beach ball.

After a few minutes, Vector checks the rearview mirror again, but he doesn't see anything.

Vector doesn't know that Dr. Nefario has positioned the ship directly *below* the escape pod.

"This is good," Gru says to Dr. Nefario. Then Gru pushes a button. A grappling hook shoots out of the side of the ship and attaches itself to Vector's pod. Now Vector can't escape.

Inside the pod, the moon has grown to the size of a small car and rolls right toward Vector!

"Aaaaaah!" cries Vector.

The now giant moon is rolling toward the girls' glass prison. Margo puts the other girls behind her to protect them.

CRASH! The moon shatters the glass, sending water everywhere. The girls leap out of the way just in time to keep from being squashed by the massive ball of rock. The moon begins to roll all over the ship, destroying everything in its path. A giant hole rips open in the wall, and the wind rushes in. The girls scream...

until they see Gru's ship below. They run to the opening.

"Mr. Gru! We're up here!" shout the girls.

Gru stands on the wing of his ship and calls up to them. "Okay, girls. You're going to have to jump!"

"Jump? Are you insane?" yells Agnes.

"Don't worry. I will catch you!" Gru promises. He holds his arms out wide.

The girls exchange nervous looks, and then Agnes and Edith jump. They land safely in Gru's arms, and he passes them down to Dr. Nefario.

"Margo, jump!" instructs Gru.

"You gave us back!" she shouts.

"I know," Gru says with remorse. "And it was the worst mistake I ever made. Margo, I promise, if you jump, I will catch you. And I will never let you go again."

Margo's heart swells a bit. She takes off her glasses and jumps blindly to Gru. He reaches out his arms and catches her, holding on tight. They're all together again. They detach the grappling hook from Vector's ship and zoom back to Earth.

Vector is on his own. The moon keeps expanding, crushing everything inside the escape pod. Vector holds on as the moon rockets into space.

Finally, the violent journey ends, and he opens his eyes. Vector realizes he's all alone on the moon, which is now back to its full size. He scratches his head. "Did not see this coming."

* * *

On that evening's newscast, there is good news to report. "This time, good triumphs, and the moon has returned to its rightful place in the sky," states the newscaster on television.

"But once again, law enforcement is baffled,

leaving the world to wonder: Who is this mysterious hero? And what will he do next?"

★ ★ ★

Back at Gru's house, it's bedtime. Gru goes
in to say good night to the girls, but they have a
request for a bedtime story.

"*Sleepy Kittens*!" they beg.

Gru gives them a funny look. "I already
picked out a book," he says.

The girls can't believe Gru has brought a
book. He reaches into his coat pocket and pulls
it out. It's called *One Big Unicorn.*

Agnes is delighted. "This is going to be the
best book ever!"

Gru reads the book, then stands up and
turns out the light. But then he pauses in the
doorway. Surprising himself, he walks back to
Agnes and gives her a kiss good night. He kisses

Edith. Then he bends down to kiss Margo, who gives him a big hug in return. Gru is shocked, and then he smiles warmly.

* * *

The next day, the three girls stand behind the curtain on the stage inside Gru's underground lab. Classical music begins to play as the curtain opens to reveal Margo, Edith, and Agnes looking splendid in their ballerina costumes. The girls start to dance, just as they did in the recital...but this time with big smiles because their special guest is in the front row.

From the audience, Gru looks on proudly. Next to him sits his mother and behind him, every single minion.

"Nice work, Gru," his mother says. "You turned out to be a great parent, just like me."

Gru decides not to point out how wrong

she is. Instead, he smiles up at the girls. Agnes smiles back at him, then she motions with her hand for him to join them onstage.

Embarrassed, Gru waves her off. Margo and Edith waggle their fingers, trying to get Gru up onstage.

"Come on!" urges Margo.

"No, I'm fine," Gru responds, shyly blushing.

Margo reaches down with her arms out, and a sea of minions carries Gru forward to her. Gru tries to resist, but there is no getting out of it. He hops onto the stage, amid claps and cheers.

Gru takes a deep breath and then...leaps, twirls, and kicks right alongside the girls! The crowd goes crazy, giving them all a standing ovation. Unable to resist joining in the fun, Dr. Nefario and his Boogie Robots even sneak out from the wings and bop to the beat. It's a dance party!

With the flick of a switch, a minion sends the

stage rising up into the air. The roof slides open, revealing a huge, full moon shining above. Gru gazes up at the moon fondly and looks back down at the girls with a smile. Then the new family dances the night away.